"Dream" CD-Soundtrack
Plug in yer favorite Songs!!!

SIDE ONE

1. Dancing Queen
2. Clyde Song
3. Getdown tonight?
4. Complicated
5. Who I am

Dream CD-Soundtrack:

SIDE TWO

1. Karma
2. Skater Boi
3. Bouncin off the Ceiling
4.
5.

What are your favorite words to doodle and draw?

Hmm...?

A Poem I Daydreamed Once...

The Weirdest Daydream I Ever Had:

What do you dream early in the morning?

_____

_____

_____

_____

_____

_____

_____

_____

_____

_____

_____

_____

_____

_____

_____

_____

_____

_____

_____

+ 2 GOOD
2 BE
————
4 GOTTEN

Daydreams Starring My Friends...

Goofy Doodles of My BFFs!

DREAM

DATES

My daydreams feature ALL my fave guys, gals, and places:

Movie guy: _____

Movie gal: _____

Movie setting: _____

Movie or TV pet: _____

TV guy: Yannick Bisson _____

TV gal: _____

TV living space: _____

TV job: _____

Singer guy: _____

Singer gal: _____

Band: _____

Sports hero: _____

Sports heroine: _____

Sports team: _____

Superhero: _____

Superheroine: _____

Y-R-U always chasin' rainbows?

My Wish List

More cheese!

HOW TO DOODLE THE PERFECT POODLE

A. POODLE

1.
2.
3.
4.
5.

B. KITTY

1.
2.
3.
4.
5.

and other animals

Cool!

C. PIGGY

1.

2.

3.

4.

5.

D. TURKEY

1.

2.

3.

4.

5.

Practice Your Pet Doodles **HERE!**

Dream the IMPOSSIBLE Dream

This is what I'd do with a million dollars:

This is where I'd go if I didn't have to be in School:

This is how I'd live if I lived on the moon:

This is where I'd go if I had my own airplane:

This is what I'd say if I met my idol:

Doodle on this page with your eyes closed.

Perfect!

Doodle With Your
Left Hand Only. ↘

← Doodle With Your
Right Hand Only.

Clock it!

WRITE for 10 minutes about the daydream you are having right now, YES, at this very minute, right NOW.............................GO!

_____
_____
_____
_____
_____
_____
_____
_____
_____
_____
_____
_____
_____
_____
_____
_____
_____
_____
_____
_____
_____
_____

What would you plant here?

The BEST Daydream I Ever Had:

_____

_____

_____

_____

_____

_____

_____

_____

_____

_____

_____

_____

_____

_____

_____

_____

_____

_____

_____

_____

Finish the doodles, and what do you see?

Daydreamin'?

Poof! — Poof! Poof! Poof! Poof!

Daydreamin'?

SENSE-sational!

Sound, Sight, Smell, Taste, and... Touch

5 Sounds I ♥

_____
_____
_____
_____
_____

5 things I ♥ To Touch

_____
_____
_____
_____
_____

5 Sights I ♥ To See

_____
_____
_____
_____
_____

5 Smells I ♥

5 things I ♥ to Taste

_____
_____
_____
_____
_____

What else do I daydream about that sounds, feels, tastes, smells, and looks good?

Even More Funny Faces

Some examples...

Hey!!

Daydreams I Have Had More Than Once:

Dream Weaver

Action!

Write a daydream about the Movie of your life!

_____

_____

_____

_____

_____

_____

_____

_____

_____

_____

_____

_____

_____

_____

_____

_____

_____

_____

_____

_____

_____

_____

WHO WILL ★ IN IT?

Cast sheet for the movie of my life

Me _____

Mom _____

Dad _____

Bro _____

Sis _____

Grandma _____

Best pal _____

Teacher _____

Neighbor _____

Pet _____

This is what I doodle

when I talk on the telephone :

Ta-Da-Daydream!
What if I had Magical powers?

Great...!

ZAP!

My Dream Menu

MENU

Appetizers: _____
_____

1st course: _____
_____

2nd course: _____
_____

3rd course: _____
_____

Dessert: _____
_____

Drinks: _____
_____

Doodle - oh - dee - dooooooooo!

DOODLE CROSSING

Travel Doodles

The top ten places I dream about visiting in the world!

1. _____
2. _____
3. _____
4. _____
5. _____
6. _____
7. _____
8. _____
9. _____
10. _____

Daydreamin'

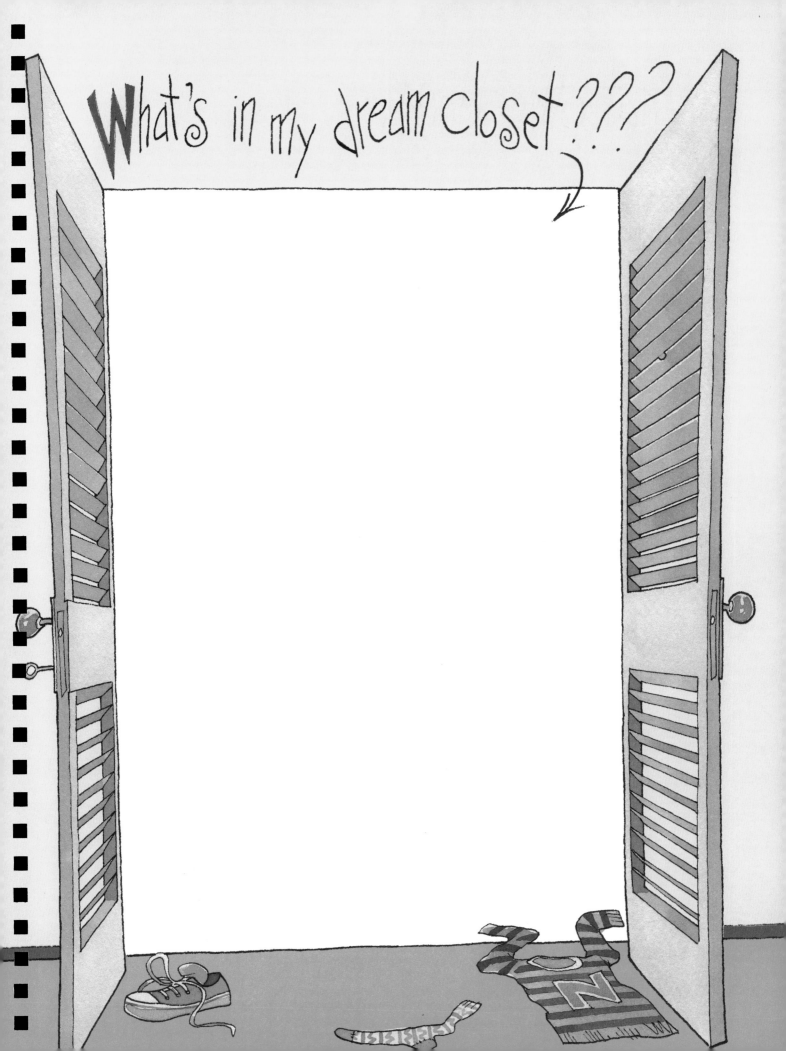

What's in my dream closet ???

What other doodle...

...is in your noodle?

BRAIN POWER!

Write a love letter to a Secret Someone

S.W.A.K.!

Dear _____

_____

_____

_____

_____

_____

_____

_____

_____

_____

_____

_____

_____

_____

_____

_____

Love, _____

Dream on...

When I am Sad, I DAYDREAM _____

_____

_____

_____

When I am angry, I DAYDREAM _____

_____

_____

_____

When I am bored, I DAYDREAM _____

_____

_____

_____

When I am psyched, I DAYDREAM _____

_____

_____

_____

A daydream I once had that came true

MORE Finish the Doodles

Make a Crowd scene! Who's here?

One last daydream...

until tomorrow!